The Adventures of Rocket Kid

tia publishing

Simon Morse

When most kids are asleep at night
And tucked up in their bed,
Jimmy runs around his room
With a colander on his head!

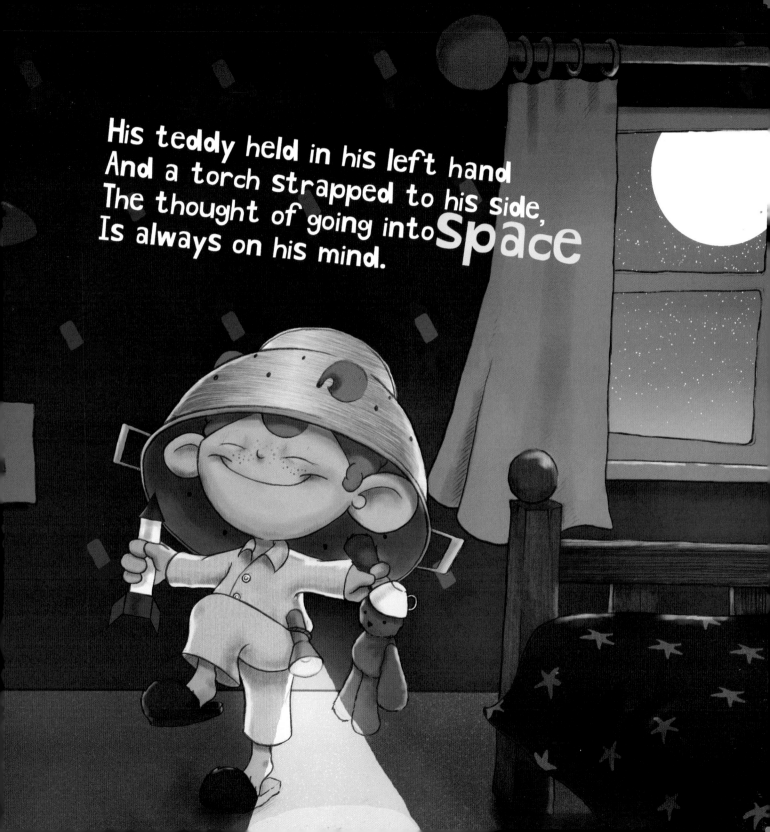

His teddy held in his left hand
And a torch strapped to his side,
The thought of going into Space
Is always on his mind.

Across the street from Jimmy, lives
A boy whose name is Sully.
He says "you'll never get to space!"
He's the biggest baddest bully!

Sometimes Jimmy gets upset,
And starts to feel quite low.
He thinks, how will I get to space?
I really do not know.

Jimmy's mum always says to him,
"Cheer up and don't be glum.
With hard work and
determination
You will get there son".

Jimmy thought really hard about
The words his mum had said.
Lots of different ideas
Started rushing through his
head!

He ran up to his room
And got some paper from his pack,
Then drew a special rocket
He could strap onto his back.

Jimmy went to bed that night
Excited by his plan.
As he fell asleep he thought,
I can get to space, I can!

Then suddenly Jimmy woke up,
And much to his surprise
His rocket pack was sitting there,

Without a second thought, he ran
And grabbed his teddy bear,
Put the colander on his head
Which messed up all his hair!

He strapped the rocket to his back,
Then quickly ran outside
And shot into the dark night sky
Holding teddy to his side.

He quickly flew around the moon
Looking for a place to land.
Far in the distance he could see
A world covered in blue sand!

He thought, wow! That looks perfect,
I'll land there to explore.
I might meet an alien,
I haven't met one before.

The planet seemed deserted
So Jimmy looked around,
Then a group of friendly faces
Popped out of the ground.

Jimmy was so excited,
And he felt over the moon!
But he could tell from Stan's sad face,
That he was filled with gloom.

"Every day we have a race
To catch stars from the stream.
The first of us to get to ten
Wins a cosmic ice cream!"

"Bobby's got more arms than me,
And Jack is really fast.
Every day we have a race
And every day I'm last!"

Jimmy remembered the words that
His mum had said to him.
He turned to Stan and said,
"There's no need to look so grim".

"Let's think very carefully,
And create a clever plan.
With **hard work and determination**

You can win the race
you can!"

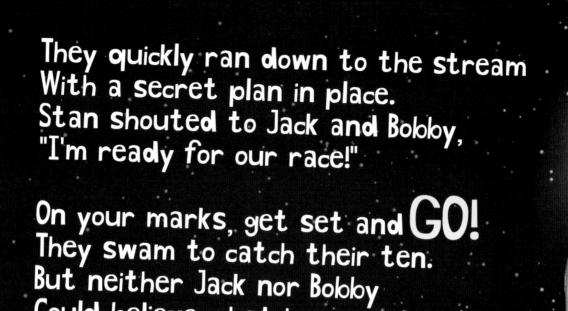

They quickly ran down to the stream
With a secret plan in place.
Stan shouted to Jack and Bobby,
"I'm ready for our race!"

On your marks, get set and GO!
They swam to catch their ten.
But neither Jack nor Bobby
Could believe what happened then.

Stan grabbed Jimmy's colander
And took it off his head.
He jumped into the flowing stream
And scooped along the edge.

Before Jack or Bobby
Could even blink an eye,

Stan had a massive pile of stars
About a metre high!

"Well every day is good", said Stan,
"But you should get home soon.
Thanks a bunch for helping me,
But you should be in your room."

Jimmy turned to set off home,
And put his rocket on his back.
He said bye to his new friends,
Stan, Bobby and Jack.

Then
WHOOSH!!!
He shot off quickly,
And flew around the moon.
All the way back to Earth
Landing safely in his room.

Jimmy climbed back into bed
With a big smile on his face!
I was sure I'd get there someday
And explore outer space!

As he fell fast asleep
With teddy tucked in nice and tight,
He dreamt about the amazing trip
That he'd been on that night.

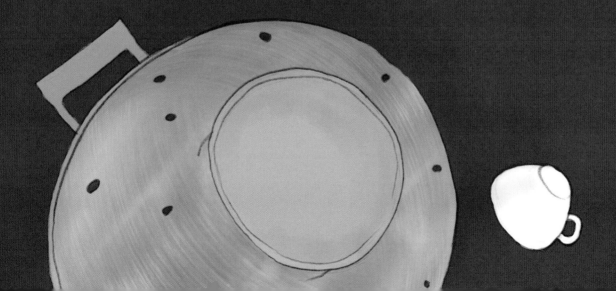

The next day on the way to school,
As Jimmy walked past Sully.
He turned around and looked at him
And said "Don't be a **bully!**"

What can you remember?

- Why was Jimmy sad?

- What does teddy wear on his head?

- What happened when Jimmy got to space?

- What did Stan want to win?

- Is there anywhere you dream of going?

- What is a bully?

tia publishing ltd
Units C and D,
Halesfield 14,
Telford,
Shropshire
TF7 4QR
www.tiapublishing.com

Printed in the UK by eniprint ltd
www.eniprint.co.uk